Goodbye, Mitch

Ruth Wallace-Brodeur   Illustrated by Kathryn Mitter

ALBERT WHITMAN & COMPANY • MORTON GROVE, ILLINOIS

For Boggart, Dexter, Eudora, and Mandy.
For Mike, Tasha, and Maggie. R.W-B.

To my mother, the very first artist who inspired me. K.M.

This story was first published, as "Maggie and Mitch,"
in the October 1993 issue of *Cricket* magazine.

The illustrations were done in watercolor and colored pencil.
The text typeface is Weideman Medium.

Text copyright © 1995 by Ruth Wallace-Brodeur.
Illustrations copyright © 1995 by Kathryn Mitter.
Published in 1995 by Albert Whitman & Company,
6340 Oakton Street, Morton Grove, Illinois 60053-2723.
Published simultaneously in Canada
by General Publishing, Limited, Toronto.
Printed in the United States of America.
10 9 8 7 6 5 4 3 2 1

Library of Congress Cataloging-in-Publication Data
Wallace-Brodeur, Ruth.
Goodbye, Mitch / Ruth Wallace-Brodeur ;
illustrated by Kathryn Mitter.
p.   cm.
Summary: A young boy describes how he feels
when the family cat dies.
ISBN 0-8075-2996-6
[1.Cats--Fiction. 2. Pets--Fiction. 3. Death--Fiction.]
I. Mitter, Kathryn, ill. II. Title.
PZ7.W15883Gr 1995   94-34656
[E]--dc20   CIP
                                                    AC

My cat Mitch stopped eating on a Sunday. I know because it was my turn to feed him.

I'd had Mitch always. We have pictures of him guarding me in my stroller. He slept on my bed every night. Mitch and I even had the same color hair. The color of marmalade, Mom says, though Mitch's was striped. Dad called us M & M . . . Michael and Mitch.

Mitch always waited in the corner by the cupboards for his breakfast and his supper. He waited there other times, too, hoping someone would feed him again.

That Sunday morning Mitch wasn't there. "Here, Mitch," I called when I put down his bowl. "Time to eat."

Mitch didn't come running down the stairs. He didn't hurry in from the living room. And he wasn't outside waiting by the door.

I found Mitch curled up in his favorite place on the back of the sofa. When I picked him up he purred and rubbed his nose under my chin.

I carried him into the kitchen. "Look, Mitch," I said. "Fish Feast with cantaloupe seeds on top." Mitch especially loved cantaloupe seeds. He looked them over, then turned back toward the living room.

"What's the matter, Mitch?" I said. "Are you getting to be like Tandy?" Tandy is my friend Lisa's cat. The only thing in the whole world that Tandy will eat is Purrfect Liver and Cheese Bits. She won't even eat real liver or cheese—just those little dried things.

Mitch didn't want his supper that night, either. Dad thought maybe he'd eaten a mouse. Mom said he hadn't been eating much of anything lately.

Mitch didn't eat on Monday or Tuesday. On Wednesday Lisa brought over some Purrfect Liver and Cheese Bits. Mitch poked at them with his nose, then turned his head away.

"He must be sick," Lisa said.

That afternoon Mom took Mitch to the vet. When she got home, she went to her study and shut the door. Mitch climbed up on the sofa and fell asleep.

After awhile, Mom called me. She looked very serious.

"Michael," she said, "Dr. Bloom thinks Mitch might have a tumor. She doesn't recommend surgery. It probably wouldn't help for long, and it would be painful."

"What are we going to do?" I asked.

"I think we'll just leave him alone," said Mom. "He seems to be comfortable."

"Will he get better?" I asked.

Mom was slow to answer. "I don't think so," she said at last. "Mitch is old. He may be getting ready to die."

"Can't we give him some medicine?"

Mom shook her head. "Only if he's in pain," she said. "There's no medicine that will make Mitch get better."

How could Mom not do anything? How could she just let this happen?

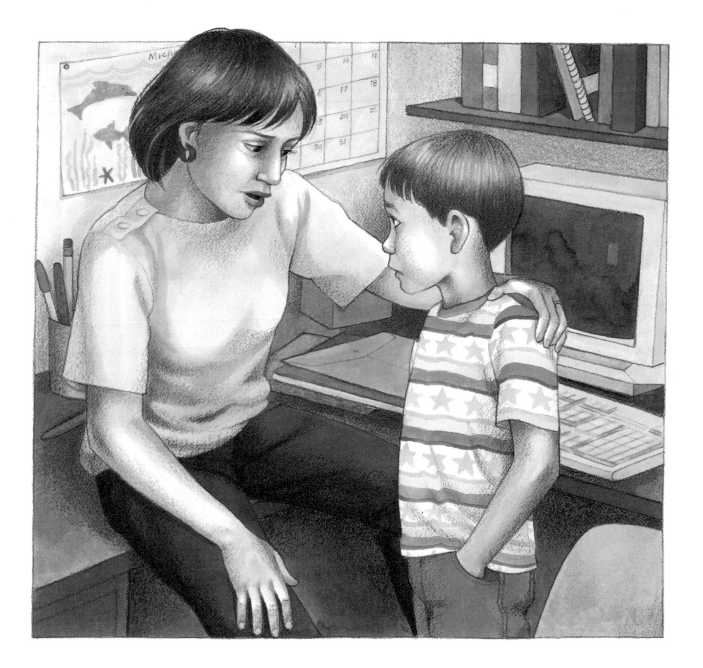

I spent the rest of the day in my room. I wanted to be alone; I didn't even want to see Lisa. Tandy was seventeen years old and perfectly all right. Mitch was only fifteen.

When I was brushing my teeth that night, Mitch came in as usual and jumped up on the edge of the sink. "Want a drink, Mitch?" I turned the faucet to just a trickle. Mitch caught a drop on his paw and licked it off. Then he tipped his head and caught more drops with flicks of his tongue. Mitch always liked to drink from a faucet better than from a bowl.

Mitch didn't eat or drink anything on Thursday or Friday, but on Saturday morning he was waiting by the cupboards when I came down for breakfast. I opened a can of tuna fish and drained the water into his bowl. Mitch always liked that better than anything. He lapped and lapped until it was all gone.

"Mom!" I yelled. "Mitch is hungry!" I put some of the tuna fish into his bowl. Mitch ate a tiny bite, then another. He ate four bites before he went into the living room. He jumped up on the couch and washed his paws and his face.

"Look, Dad," I said. "Mitch is better!"

We all stood there, smiling and watching Mitch. Mom rubbed her face in his fur. "Good old Mitch," she said. Mitch patiently licked smooth the fur she had mussed. Just like always.

Mitch had a little egg the next Tuesday. He drank more tuna water on
Thursday. Every night he jumped up on the edge of the sink while I brushed
my teeth. Sometimes he caught a few drops of water. Mostly he just watched.

Mitch was still silky and soft. But he felt all skinny and bumpy with
bones when I picked him up. His breath smelled bad when he yawned

or rubbed his nose under my chin.

Saturday afternoon Mitch asked to go out. He hadn't been outside in over two weeks, except to visit the vet. He blinked and stretched in the warm spring sun. Then he rolled on his back in the dust, stopping to watch things upside down, just like always.

Lisa came over then, and I didn't see where Mitch went. He wasn't back at suppertime. I called and called at bedtime, but no Mitch.

"Did Mitch come back?" I asked first thing the next morning.

"No, Michael." Dad cleared his throat. "You know," he said, "sometimes cats go away to die. They seem to want to be alone. It's sad for us, but we want Mitch to do what's best for him."

How could being alone now be best for Mitch?

"It's true," Lisa said on the telephone. "My grandma's cat went off and died, and she never found him. My mom says it's easier that way since you don't have to watch. But Grandma said she never got over wondering."

I didn't want to upset Mitch, but I kept looking for him, just in case. Monday morning there he was, sitting on the porch waiting to be let in. He wobbled when he walked past his bowl and into the living room. He sat by the sofa and looked at his favorite place. I picked him up and whispered, "I'm glad you came home," before I put him on his cushion.

Mitch slept on the back of the sofa all that day. He showed up at the bathroom door when I was brushing my teeth at bedtime, but he couldn't jump up onto the sink. He just stared at the cup of water I put down for him.

"Come on, Mitch," I said and carried him to bed. He slept very close to me, purring whenever I woke up and patted him.

In the morning I found Mitch behind the bathroom door. "I think he likes the heat from the shower," Mom said. We put down an old sweatshirt for him to lie on.

Mitch slept in the bathroom for two days. He blinked and purred whenever he noticed us. On Thursday he didn't open his eyes much. I sat next to him a lot. I think he liked that because every time I came, he put his paw on my hand and pulled himself up against it. I was getting used to having hard bubbles roll up my throat and make me cry. After I cried, I would feel better, just sitting there with Mitch.

Thursday night when I went to see Mitch, he stretched his head up toward me and meowed. I thought he felt cold, so I got a blanket and wrapped him up. I sat with him all wrapped up like that in the rocking chair in Mom and Dad's room. He fell asleep with his head under my chin. We sat there a long time. I tried not to move. After awhile, Mitch gave a big, shuddery sigh. His head slipped down on my chest.

"There, there," I whispered. "Don't be scared, Mitch, don't be scared." He gave one more sigh, and then was still.

I just stayed there until I could call Mom. She touched Mitch very gently. He didn't breathe. He didn't move. "Do you want me to take him, Michael?" she said softly.

I shook my head. "Not yet," I said. "Not yet."

Mom got Dad, and they sat on the bed and waited until I was ready to put Mitch down.

We wrapped him in the old sweatshirt and put him in a
cardboard box.

The next morning Dad dug a hole at the back of the garden,
and we buried Mitch.

I think about Mitch a lot. Sometimes I cry, but I feel good, too. I'm glad he was my cat. And I'm glad I was holding him when he died. Lisa and I planted some flowers next to where he's buried.

I'll always remember Mitch. I'll always love him, too.